A Max & Colby
Max's Big Adventure

Janis Hennessey

Illustrated by Teresa Street

ISBN
ISBN

To Julian and Luke – jh
To Marcus and Veronica – ts
Happy & loving children

Max and Colby are best friends. They play together and they care about each other especially when one of them is in danger.

1. Friendship - Fiction, 2. Animals - Dogs, Ages: 2 - 8

BigTree Press
55 Applevale Drive
Dover, NH 03820
USA

Table of Contents

"Max's Big Adventure" is the third of the Max & Colby adventures.

We welcome you to check out the other stories at **Amazon.com.**

All books by Janis Hennessey are on page 40.

During the night it snowed and snowed.

By morning the snow had stopped and Max and Colby were ready for the day.

"Colby, Colby! Come and see what I found!" Max barked with lots of enthusiasm.

"Look, Colby, the snow made a path over the fence.
Let's leave the yard and have an adventure!" said
Max happily.

"NO!! NO!! Max! Do NOT go over the fence. Colby was afraid of what might happen to them.

"Stay here. Stay in the yard with me!" said Colby. He was not happy. He did not want to leave the yard to have an adventure.

"Oh Colby, I want to run and play in the woods with you. It will be lots of fun," urged Max.

"COLBY, COME AND FOLLOW ME!"
Max barked.

But, Max did not listen to Colby. Instead, he flew up the path of snow to the top of the fence.

He stood there for just a moment looking around. Then...

he JUMPED over the fence!

"Look, Colby! I am OUT! This is fun!" Max was so proud of himself.

Max ran and jumped in and out of the drifts of snow. He looked like a black, brown and white bunny playing in the snow.

"BARK! BARK! BARK! Bark! Max was now deep in the woods.

After a while, Colby lay down in the snow by the back gate but he did not take a nap.

He waited............
        and waited............
                and waited............
                        hoping that Max would return.

All of a sudden,

one of Colby's ears perked up. He heard something!
"Bark!"

"BARK! BARK! BARK! BARK! BARK! Look, Colby, I AM BACK!" Max was so very happy to see Colby.

Max told Colby all about his adventures. "In the woods when I stopped running and jumping, I was cold.

I ate the snow, but I was still hungry.

There were no animals to play with me, so I was all alone. I was sad, because you were not with me.

I was scared that I was lost, but my NOSE knew how to get me home."
Colby listened quietly to Max.

Then Colby shouted happily to Max, "*Jump* back over the fence!"

So, Max jumped, jumped, jumped, jumped and jumped.

"I can't jump over the fence! It's too high. And, there s no path of snow back over the fence.

Open the gate for me. I am cold. I want to come home," said a very tired Max.

"Oh, Max, I can't open the gate. I don't know how," explained Colby. "You have to jump back over the fence."

"I do not know what to do. Max, I can't help you," said Colby. He was very upset.

HONK! HONK! The family was home.
Colby turned.

And, then he

RAN and BARKED all the way to the front gate.

Max also saw the family car. He *JUMPED* and BARKED behind the back gate.

After Jared got out of the car, he saw Colby running toward him.

"Hi, Colby!" said Jared. "I hear Max, but I don't see him. Where is he?"

"Oh, now I see him!" said Jared.

He hurried behind Colby to help Max.

After Jared quickly pushed the snow out of the way, he opened the gate!

Both dogs were so excited, they JUMPED all over Jared! They all fell into the snow.

Colby and Max raced Jared all the way into the house.

Jared fed both hungry dogs a big delicious dinner.

After eating, the two dogs lay down on the rug for a nice warm nap. Max was so tired that he fell right to sleep.

Before closing his eyes, Colby noticed

it had started to snow.... **again!**

Draw a *happy* picture of Max and Colby playing around a snowman or a snowdog.

Draw a *quiet* picture of Max and Colby taking a nap somewhere inside the house.

Acknowledgments

I would like to thank each of the wonderful members of my family and friends who assisted me in writing this story. I so appreciated their excellent suggestions and their constant support.

Family: My husband, Barry Hennessey, our three children and their spouses, Evan & Jenn Hennessey, Meg & Chris Scull, Jared & Liz Hennessey, my sister, brother and sister-in-law, Karen, Bill & Jody Dieruf.

Teachers: Mary Chamberlain, Jennifer Connelly, Faith Garnett, Stacey Kostis, Lauren Schultz, Ann Marie Staples, Linda Petersen.

Children's librarians: Debra Cheney, Laura Horan, Linda Smart, Susan Williams. Thanks for field testing each story with young school children. Your feedback was so valuable.

Special thanks to Victor López for all his tech magic in getting the book ready.

I applaud and deeply thank Teresa Street for putting her heart and soul into illustrating all the "Max & Colby Adventures". Her creative talent put life into the backyard antics of two dogs. Teresa and I are a perfect pair because we are the grandmothers of Marcus who knew all the animals in all the stories.

About the Author

Janis Hennessey, along with her husband and three children, have hosted many pets, including dogs, cats, birds, fish, gerbils, rabbits and even snakes, in their New Hampshire home.

At the age of 10 Janis began writing neighborhood plays for her friends in Louisville, Kentucky. Over the years these stories evolved into various children's books. She loves to use the real stories of the family pets and the children in her stories.

Janis earned a master's degree in French Literature from University of Kentucky and a diploma in French History from the Sorbonne, Université de Paris. She taught French in Kentucky, Massachusetts, and New Hampshire where she encouraged her students to write creatively in another language.

About the Illustrator

Teresa Street, a New Hampshire native, is primarily a self-taught artist. She worked with various artists from Texas and from New Hampshire as well as studied art at the University of New Hampshire. She is a past member of the Durham Art Association and has done commissioned portraits.

Teresa first met the author many years ago when they welcomed their first grandchild, Marcus. A collaboration ensued to bring Janis' stories to life. The fourth and fifth books add Teresa's family pets into the Max and Colby's adventures. Her rich and creative illustrations have been a labor of love for the children, grandchildren and family pets.

Books by Janis Hennessey

Amazon.com   janishennessey.com   @janishennesseyauthor

A Max & Colby Adventure:
Ages: 4 - 6

1. "Zooming Fun!"
2. "A New Dog?"
3. "Max's Big Adventure"
4. "Lost !"
5. "Who Is UP In OUR TREE?"
6. "Shadow Catchers"

The Why Did series:
Ages: 4 - 6

1. "Why Did Marcus Go To The Restaurant?"
2. "Why Did Emma Make Teddy Bear Bread?"
3. "Why Did Kaden Accept The Challenge?"

The 3Ds:
Ages: 8 - 10

1. "The Mystery Of The Lost Ring"
2. "The Mystery Of The Skull And The Hidden Past"
3. "The Mystery At The End Of Willow Street"

Books In French: **Why Did:** « Pourquoi Emma a-t-il fait un Nounours en Pain Brioché ? »

Max & Colby:

1. « A Toute Vitesse !! »
2. « Un Nouveau Chien ? »
3. « La Grande Aventure de Max »
4. « Qui est dans NOTRE Arbre? »
5. « Perdu »
6. « L' Attrape-ombre »

Made in the USA
Middletown, DE
13 March 2025

72630312R00026